The United States

South Carolina

Paul Joseph
ABDO & Daughters

visit us at
www.abdopub.com

Published by Abdo & Daughters, 4940 Viking Drive, Suite 622, Edina, Minnesota 55435.
Copyright © 1998 by Abdo Consulting Group, Inc., Pentagon Tower, P.O. Box 36036, Minneapolis, Minnesota 55435 USA. International copyrights reserved in all countries. No part of this book may be reproduced in any form without written permission from the publisher.

Printed in the United States.

Cover and Interior Photo credits: Peter Arnold, Inc., Superstock, Archive, Corbis-Bettmann, Allsport USA

Edited by Lori Kinstad Pupeza
Contributing editor Brooke Henderson
Special thanks to our Checkerboard Kids—Francesca Tuminelly, John Hansen, Raymond Sherman

All statistics taken from the 1990 census; The Rand McNally Discovery Atlas of The United States.

Library of Congress Cataloging-in-Publication Data

Joseph, Paul, 1970-
     South Carolina / Paul Joseph.
     p. cm. -- (United States)
     Includes index.
     Summary: Surveys the people, geography, and history of the southeastern Palmetto State.
     ISBN 1-56239-876-8
     1. South Carolina--Juvenile literature. [South Carolina.] I. Title. II. Series: United States (Series)
     F269.3.J68 1998
     975.7--dc21   97-21418
                                                     CIP
                                                     AC

Contents

Welcome to South Carolina

The wonderful state of South Carolina is shaped like a rough triangle. It can be found on the southeastern coast of the United States bordering the Atlantic Ocean.

South Carolina is loaded with forests, swamps, lakes, rivers, and mountains. The beautiful state is a popular vacation getaway for thousands of people each year. The resorts have beaches, golf courses, tennis courts, and many other things to do.

South Carolina also has a very rich and long history. It was a major battleground of the **American Revolution**. It also was nearly destroyed in the **Civil War**.

South Carolina was the first state to break away from the United States. It was part of the **Confederacy**. States belonging to the Confederacy wanted to keep the southern **tradition** of slavery. This was one of the reasons for the **Civil War** between the northern states and the southern states.

In the end, the northern states won the Civil War and South Carolina had to begin rebuilding its state. It took many years and cost a lot of money.

Today, the state is thriving. It is an **industrial** leader in **manufacturing**. **Tourism** is also a big industry in South Carolina. Now the state is part of what people call the "New South."

Cypress Gardens in South Carolina.

Fast Facts

South Carolina is one of the original 13 colonies

SOUTH CAROLINA

Capital and Largest city
Columbia (99,052 people)

Area
30,207 square miles
(78,236 sq km)

Population
3,505,707 people
Rank: 25th

Statehood
May 23, 1788
(8th state admitted)

Principal rivers
Savannah River, Pee Dee River

Highest point
Sassafras Mountain;
3,560 feet (1,085 m)

Motto
Animis opibusque parati
(Prepared in mind and resources)
and *Dum spiro spero* (While I
breathe, I hope)

Song
"South Carolina on my mind"

Famous People
Mary McLeod Bethune, John C.
Calhoun, Robert Mills

*Y*ellow Jessamine

*S*tate Flag

*P*almetto

*C*arolina Wren

About South Carolina

The Palmetto State

Detail area

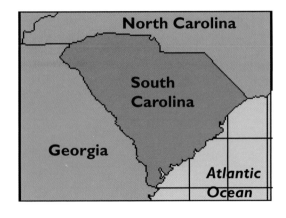

North Carolina

South Carolina

Georgia

Atlantic Ocean

SC

South Carolina's abbreviation

Borders: west (Georgia), north (North Carolina), east (North Carolina, Atlantic Ocean), south (Atlantic Ocean, Georgia)

Nature's Treasures

South Carolina has many wonderful treasures in its state. There are scenic mountains, many lakes and rivers, incredible beaches, forests, and the Atlantic Ocean.

On the coast of South Carolina the weather is wonderful. It makes great vacation spots for people in the winter. Except in the higher mountains, the summers in South Carolina are very warm.

Another treasure of South Carolina is the forests. Forests cover nearly 65 percent of the state's land! South Carolina also has a great variety of wildlife.

The land of South Carolina offers excellent farming. The state ranks among the top ten in the country for producing peanuts, peaches, and tobacco. Stone and clay are the main minerals found in the state. They come from deep in the ground.

Not too many states offer as many different treasures from nature as South Carolina. The main reason people live in this state and visit it is because of the wonderful treasures.

The White-Water Falls are on the border between North Carolina and South Carolina.

Beginnings

The earliest known people to have lived in South Carolina were **Native Americans**. Many different groups of Native Americans lived in the state.

Europeans tried to **settle** the area in 1526 and later in 1562, but did not succeed. In 1670, the English started the first permanent European settlement in the state. In 1680, it was named Charles Town in honor of King Charles II.

In 1778, the state wanted to be on its own and declared independence from England. From that came the **American Revolution**.

Many battles took place on South Carolina soil during the American Revolution. After America won the war, South Carolina began to prosper. On May 23, 1788, South Carolina officially entered the Union and became the eighth state. The cotton gin had been invented and the state grew wealthy raising cotton.

In 1860, South Carolina became the first of 11 states to leave the Union. By 1861, the **Civil War** began. This was a war between the northern states and the southern states. The South lost and South Carolina suffered greatly.

Fort Sumter in Charleston, South Carolina.

South Carolina was readmitted to the Union in June of 1868. The state rebuilt itself steadily and began to prosper again. This time it was with **textile** mills and farming.

B.C. to 1600s

Early South Carolina

During the Ice Age, many thousands of years ago, South Carolina was covered by huge glaciers of ice. Many years later the ice began to melt and the land formed.

The first known people to live in the area were **Native Americans**.

1562: Jean Ribault sets up a French colony at Port Royal.

1670: The first permanent English **settlement** in South Carolina was started in 1680. It was named Charles Town.

South Carolina

B.C. to 1600s

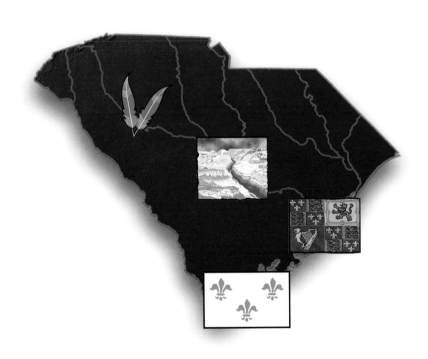

1700s to 1800s

Statehood

 1776: South Carolina declares its independence from England.

 1783: Charles Town is renamed Charleston.

 1788: South Carolina becomes the eighth state on May 23.

 1790: The capital is moved to its present day home of Columbia.

 1846: William Gregg builds a cotton mill at Graniteville.

South Carolina

1700s to 1800s

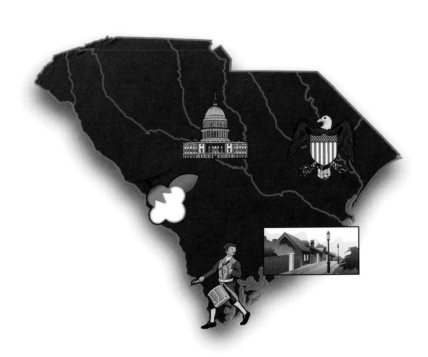

1860 to Now

Civil War to Present Day

 1860: South Carolina is the first southern state to leave the Union.

 1865: Union troops burn down Columbia.

 1868: South Carolina is readmitted to the Union.

 1952: Clark Hills Dam is completed.

 1989: Hurricane Hugo devastates the state, leaving six billion dollars in damage and 29 deaths.

South Carolina

1860 to Now

South Carolina's People

There are about 3.5 million people living in the state of South Carolina. The first known people to live in South Carolina were **Native Americans**. Today, only a small percentage of Native Americans live in the state.

Many notable people have made South Carolina home. John C. Calhoun was vice president of the United States from 1825 to 1833. Born in Abbeville County, Calhoun graduated from Yale and became a lawyer. He was also a **congressman**, **senator**, secretary of war, and secretary of state.

Another well-known national figure from South Carolina is Strom Thurmond. Thurmond was born in Edgefield in 1902. He was a judge, a major general in World War II, and governor of South Carolina. In 1948, he was the controversial Dixiecrat candidate for president of the United States. He has been a **senator** since 1954. At the age of 94, he is still going strong as the senator from South Carolina.

Other notables of South Carolina are heavyweight boxing champion Joe Frazier, minister and **civil rights** activist Benjamin E. Mays, naval hero Robert Smalls, popular children's author Betsy Byars, and basketball star Kevin Garnett.

John C. Calhoun

Kevin Garnett

Strom Thurmond

Splendid Cities

South Carolina has many splendid cities in its state. Although not one city in the state has 100,000 people living in it, there are still many things to do and places to see.

The capital and largest city in South Carolina is Columbia. There are just under 100,000 people living in the city. Columbia is located in almost the exact center of the state. The city is also filled with museums, historic sites, and is home to the University of South Carolina.

The historic city of Charleston is near the Atlantic Ocean. The second largest city in the state, Charleston, is known as a military town. It has navy, air force, and missile bases.

Greenville

Spartanburg

Columbia

Charleston

It is also known for its famed military academy, the Citadel.

Charleston sits on a narrow **peninsula** between the Cooper and Ashley rivers. These two rivers and the Atlantic Ocean give Charleston one of the largest seaports in the United States.

Greenville and Spartanburg are **industrial** cities. Some of the industries in these cities are **textile** mills, metalworks, machinery, and office furniture. They also are known for growing peaches.

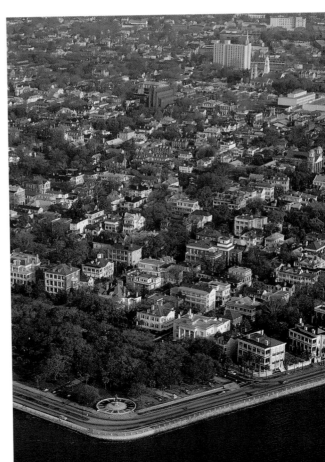

Charleston, South Carolina.

South Carolina's Land

South Carolina has some of the most beautiful and diverse land in the country. It has mountains, lakes, deep forests, and sandy beaches on the Atlantic Ocean. The state is divided into three different regions.

The Coastal Plain covers more than half the state and is also called "low country." It goes from the ocean to the middle of the state. It has sandy beaches on the coast and rich swamplands inland.

The Coastal Plain has always had large **plantations**. First there were rice plantations, then **indigo**, then cotton, and now tobacco.

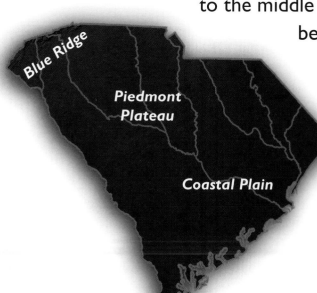

Blue Ridge

Piedmont Plateau

Coastal Plain

The Piedmont Plateau covers the rest of the state except for the very northwestern tip. This area is also called "up country."

The land in the Piedmont Plateau is very rocky. A few single hills, called monadnocks, stand out. Some of them are named the Kings Mountain, Paris Mountain, and Table Rock.

The Blue Ridge region in the northwestern corner of the state covers only 500 square miles (1295 sq km). Here, almost on the North Carolina border, is the highest point in the state. Sassafras Mountain is 3,560 feet (1,085 m) tall.

The Blue Ridge Mountains in South Carolina.

South Carolina at Play

There are many fun resorts in the state. The most famous in South Carolina is Hilton Head. Hilton Head Island has been a year-round resort since the late 1950s. The Island has miles of beaches, golf courses, and other fun activities.

South Carolina is known for its state parks system. There is one state park within an hour's drive from every home in the state. Some of the parks are the Fort Sumter National Monument, Cowpens National Battlefield, and Kings Mountain National Military Park.

Many tourists visit South Carolina for its famous gardens. Near Charleston is the world-famous Middleton Place Gardens. These gardens were laid out by slaves in 1741, making them the oldest gardens in the United States.

In the cities are museums, art fairs, and festivals. People also enjoy the hills and mountains for camping and hiking. Besides the Atlantic Coast, people also play at the many lakes and rivers. There people fish, swim, and boat.

Middleton Place Gardens, the oldest gardens in the United States.

South Carolina at Work

The people of South Carolina must work to make money. Many people work in or around the cities, while others work in rural communities.

A lot of the people work in **manufacturing**. South Carolina is one of the top **textile** manufacturers in the United States. Cotton fabrics make up much of the output. South Carolina also makes fabrics such as rayon, nylon, and Orlon.

Many people in South Carolina are also farmers. There are about 25,000 farms in the state. The most valuable crops grown are tobacco and soybeans. South Carolina ranks among the top ten producing states in peaches, peanuts, tobacco, and cotton.

Some people in South Carolina are miners, Stone and clay are the chief minerals in the state.

Other people work on the coastal fisheries. Some of the shell fish caught are shrimps, crabs, and oysters.

There are many different things to do and see in the great state of South Carolina. Because of its natural beauty, people, land, mountains, and forests, South Carolina is a great place to visit, live, work, and play.

South Carolina is among the top ten peach producers in the country.

Fun Facts

• The city of Charleston was the first capital in South Carolina. The people in the up country protested that the people in the low country were controlling the state government. So in 1790, the state capital was moved from Charleston, which is located on the East Coast, to Columbia, which is in the middle of the state. Today, the capital is still Columbia.

• The first capital, Charleston, was actually named Charles Town in honor of the English King Charles II. In 1783, after the United States gained independence from England, the name was changed to Charleston.

• The highest point in the state is Sassafras Mountain. It is 3,560 feet (1,085 m) tall. The lowest point is at sea level.

•South Carolina is the 40th biggest state. Its land covers 30,207 square miles (78,236 sq km). In **population**, however, it is the 25th largest.

Hilton Head Island, South Carolina

Glossary

American Revolution: a war that gave the United States its independence from Great Britain.

Civil Rights Movement: a movement by African Americans to have the same rights as white people.

Civil War: a war between groups within the same country.

Confederacy: a group that bands together for a common belief. In this case it is the 11 southern states that left the Union between 1860 and 1861.

Congressman: a person elected by the people to represent them and make laws.

Indigo: a plant used to make a blue colored dye.

Industrial: big businesses such as factories or manufacturing.

Manufacture: to make things by machine in a factory.

Native Americans: the first people who were born in and occupied North America.

Peninsula: a long narrow piece of land that extends into the water.

Plantation: a huge farming estate that is worked on by many people.

Population: the number of people living in a certain place.

Senator: one of two elected officials from a state that represents the state in Washington, D.C. There they make laws and are part of Congress.

Settlement: a new community built by settlers.

Settlers: people that move to a new land and build a community.

Textile: a woven cloth or fabric.

Tourism: a business that serves people who are traveling for pleasure, and visiting places of interest.

Tradition: a belief or custom that is handed down from one generation to another.

Internet Sites

South Carolina State Museum!
http://www.museum.state.sc.us/
At your fingertips you'll experience the Palmetto State from the mountains to the sea—its art, history, natural history, science and technology. Whatever your interest, you'll find four large floors of exhibits to explore and enjoy. In fact the museum is located inside its largest artifact—the historic Columbia Mill building, which opened in 1894 as the world's first totally electric textile mill.

Civil War@Charleston
http://www.awod.com/gallery/probono/cwchas/cwlayout.html
For any Civil War buff this is a super interactive page. Battle scenes, biographies, military operations, historical events surrounding the war, and much more. A very interesting and informative site.

These sites are subject to change. Go to your favorite search engine and type in South Carolina for more sites.

PASS IT ON

Tell Others Something Special About Your State
To educate readers around the country, pass on interesting tips, places to see, history, and little unknown facts about the state you live in. We want to hear from you!
To get posted on ABDO & Daughters website, e-mail us at "mystate@abdopub.com"

Index